First published by Parragon in 2013
Parragon
Chartist House
15–17 Trim Street
Bath BA1 1HA, UK
www.parragon.com

Copyright © Parragon Books Ltd 2013

Written by Steve Smallman
Edited by Laura Baker
Production by Jonathan Wakeham

Illustrated by Simon Mendez
Designed by Kathryn Davies

ISBN 978-1-4723-1136-8

Printed in China

Muddypaws' New Friends

Bath · New York · Singapore · Hong Kong · Cologne · Delhi
Melbourne · Amsterdam · Johannesburg · Shenzhen

Ben and his puppy, Muddypaws, were best friends. They did everything together ...

from galloping games ...

to quiet cuddles.

But when Ben went to school,
Muddypaws had to stay at home
with nobody to play with.

Then one day, Ben said, "Come on, Muddypaws, let's go to school!" Muddypaws was very excited ...

and pulled on

his leash all the way!

But they didn't go to Ben's school. They went to ...

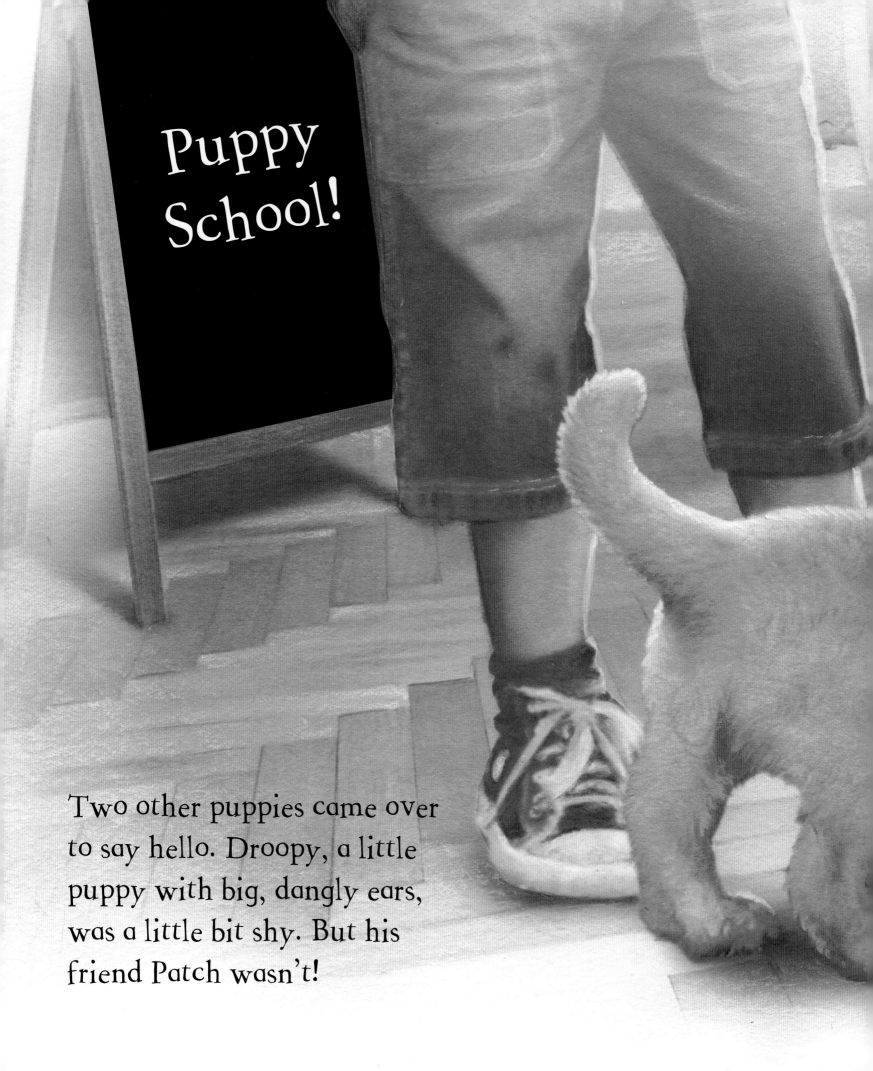

Puppy
School!

Two other puppies came over
to say hello. Droopy, a little
puppy with big, dangly ears,
was a little bit shy. But his
friend Patch wasn't!

"Muddypaws, why don't you play with your new friends till it's time to start school?" said Ben.

Ben opened the door, and the three puppies chased each other around and around the yard. Muddypaws loved having new friends to play with!

The three puppies found a big puddle.

Splish!

Droopy tiptoed in up to
the bottom of his ears.

Splash!

Muddypaws jumped
in up to his tummy.

Splosh!

Patch jumped in
up to his collar!

Then it was time to start the class.
The first lesson was "Sitting."

"SIT!"

Droopy sat.

"SIT!"

Muddypaws rolled over!
"Oh, Muddypaws," chuckled
Ben. "Nice try, but not
just right yet!"

"SIT!"

Patch shook water all over the place!

The second lesson was "Fetching." Everyone had brought a rolled-up sock for their puppies to fetch.

"Fetch!" Muddypaws and his new friends galloped off together.

Droopy picked up his sock.

Muddypaws picked up his sock, too!

Patch pounced on his. Then he shook it until it unrolled, flew up in the air, and ...

... landed on Muddypaws' head!

Muddypaws and Droopy happily trotted back together. "Good boy!" laughed Ben. "You fetched your sock, and now you look just like your friend!"

Before the end of the class, the teacher wanted to try the "Sitting" lesson again.

"SIT!"

Droopy sat.

"SIT!"

Muddypaws woofed happily. But he didn't sit.

"SIT!"

Patch chased his tail. He didn't like to sit still!

Ben thought he'd try one last time ...

"Come on, Muddypaws, you can do it.

SIT!" said Ben.

Just then, Patch ran over to get his sock back, but his leash got tangled around Ben's legs!

Ben fell on his bottom with a great big

bump!

And, because Ben was sitting down, Muddypaws sat down!

And, because their friend Muddypaws was sitting down, Droopy and Patch sat down too!

"Hurray!" cheered Ben.

"You did it!"

When it was time to go home, Muddypaws was a little bit sad to say goodbye to Droopy and Patch. "Don't worry, Muddypaws!" said Ben. "You'll see them again next week!"

So with a happy goodbye "woof," Muddypaws headed back home with Ben, his very best friend of all!